REPO
ELF

REPO ELF

A Cautionary Holiday Tale
Not Suitable for Children

10th Anniversary Second Edition

Tom Sims

Interior Illustrations by Tony Perri

REPO ELF
A CAUTIONARY HOLIDAY TALE
NOT SUITABLE FOR CHILDREN

iUniverse books may be ordered through booksellers or by contacting:

iUniverse
1663 Liberty Drive
Bloomington, IN 47403
www.iuniverse.com
1-800-Authors (1-800-288-4677)

ISBN: 978-1-5320-0778-1 (sc)
ISBN: 978-1-5320-0779-8 (e)

Print information available on the last page.

iUniverse rev. date: 09/30/2016

To Aly and Julia, my beautiful daughters.

CONTENTS

ONE

Travis Johnson's Testimony,
Part 1 of 8: Scheming to Get the Gift

Editor's Note: The following is the first testimony from Travis Johnson to the North Pole Counsel of Regional Vice Presidents, as they wanted to know more about the incident. The Counsel is a small panel made up of Santa VPs overseeing several regions (such as North America, Europe, and the Pacific Rim). Testimonies are short with many breaks in between. These breaks are for drinking hot chocolate with marshmallows and whipped cream, eating iced ginger bread cookies, and (of course) taking as many naps as necessary.

My name is Travis Johnson, and I'm ten years old. And I had to learn the hard way what my mom has told me a lot: "You have to stand up but not for yourself—for what's right. There's a big difference."

Did you ever think the kids you're hanging out with aren't any good for you—but you didn't know what to do about it? It's a pain to stand up for what's right. We all want to be liked—it's natural, my mom says. So we let people say stuff we don't agree with, and we even let them tell us we're wrong. Like they got it right and we got it wrong. Like they know better than us. Like we all don't have to learn the hard way. As if I didn't.

A couple years ago, I started playing with some other kids in my neighborhood. That's okay, but I'm not saying they're like good friends or anything. I just play basketball with them sometimes and hang out at their houses. It's something to do. I talk to my mom about her friends, and she says sometimes we make friends with people we were just meant to pass a little time with. Then they realize they're not good friends. I don't want to do that with Dirk and Angelo. My friend Chris I like spending time with. I guess there's the difference there too.

Well, one day we're all at Dirk's house. When we go to his house, he always wants to stay in the bedroom. He yells at his mom, telling her we don't want any of her snacks or lemonade. I don't say anything when he's doing this. Once, I told his mom I'd take a lemonade, and Dirk practically smacked me—grazing his hand against my arm. His face said, "Don't ask her for anything" without him saying it. What I should have said was, "Your mom is like my mom— she's nice, she wants to give us something to drink. Let her." What I said was... nothing. Like I said, it's a pain to stand up for what's right.

Dirk's bedroom smelled like dirty socks. I've never told him. I just opened a window. No matter how cold it is outside. That day, we were all talking about Christmas.

Everyone wanted something. Angelo wanted a high-hat cymbal for his drum set and Chris wanted a pink leather jacket. Oh, she's a girl—Chris, I mean. Her parents and mine were in the same bowling league, until my Dad died. Her parents are the best, still wanted her to stay in the bowling league and hang out even after Dad was gone. They hang out a lot together—so we do too. We bowled our first game together when we were three years old. But it's not like we're bowling nuts like our parents were or anything, you know.

Anyway I'm telling you nobody but nobody that year wanted a present more than Dirk. He wanted a gas-powered motor scooter. I never had one, but they looked cool.

Chris said to Dirk, "How are you going to get a scooter like that?"

"You idiot," he said to her. "I'm asking Santa for it."

We sat there quiet for a moment. If everyone else thought what I was thinking, then you'd know why we were quiet. None of us wanted to admit we believed in Santa. And Dirk just did!

"You believe in Santa?" Chris asked.

"Yeah," Dirk replied—like we were stupid for not knowing he did. "And why not? What else do I have to believe in, huh? Hey, I got news for your losers. We all better believe in Santa or we got no hope to get anything good for Christmas. What do you want for Christmas?" he asked me.

"A Z-Box."

"Who doesn't," Dirk said. "They're not cheap. Better get writing to Santa, and you better start acting the part."

Angelo laughed a little, "What's that mean?"

Dirk sneered, "Better start acting like you care. Doing the dishes, being all polite, you know?"

"Who says it's an act?" Chris asked.

"Who says it's an act?" Dirk repeated in a high pitched voice to make fun of her. "You're such a…" he began and stopped.

Chris got up and walked to Dirk. She had done this before. "Such a what?" she asked. If there was one thing Chris hated to hear, it was that she was acting like… well, like a girl. "Go ahead," she said to Dirk, and she put her hair behind her shoulder to get it out of the way. "Say it."

He didn't respond. She punched him in the arm.

"That didn't hurt," he said and punched her back, but Chris didn't even flinch.

I could feel my heart in my chest. It's the feeling I get when I know something is wrong. Wish it would tell me what to do and not just that there's something wrong. I wanted to punch Dirk so bad for touching Chris. At the time, I didn't know what words to say. The right words to say come later, and I can't stand that about myself. My mom tells me that is completely normal, that adults feel that too. She says everyone feels that at one time or another. Whenever she says stuff like that, she also says, "Steady as a second hand." I don't know what that means. Anyway, I hope that's not the way it is when I'm older. As a grown-up, hopefully the right words to say will come to me at that time right to the person who needs to hear them.

Dirk turned back to the rest of us and said, "I put on the act last year—even took out the trash—and I got an all right present. Anyway so this year, I'm getting the scooter, I know it."

"Yeah," Angelo added. "Last year I did all my chores, didn't get any notes sent home from my teachers, and made my bed nearly every day from Thanksgiving all the way to Christmas Day." He emphasized the word *all* and dragged it out, as if four weeks felt like an entire year. "I got a snare drum. This year, I want the high-hat. I got to start getting in good with Santa."

We left Dirk's house that afternoon, and I walked Chris home. "Is your arm okay?" I asked.

"What?" she said, like she didn't know what I was talking about. "Oh, that?" she waved her hand. "That little wimp? I hurt him worse."

That year, we all must have put on a pretty good act. Angelo got his high-hat, Chris go her jacket, and I got a basketball. I knew a Z-Box was asking too much. Dirk got a scooter, but it wasn't motorized. He wasted no time that morning yelling at his parents about it.

I don't understand a kid yelling at his mom or dad. If it wasn't for them, we wouldn't have food or a bed or even the toys we wanted. His mom was nice, always wanting to make us brownies or some fruit punch. My mom worked all day or else she'd make us that stuff too.

It was a few days after Christmas, and something strange happened. Chris and I were on the swings at the playground when Dirk ran up. He had been running around all over looking for us and I guess the playground

5

wasn't his first stop. He couldn't breathe, and at first he couldn't talk.

"My scooter..." he said.

"What about it," I said.

"Stolen..." he said.

"Stolen?" Chris asked.

"Who stole it?" I asked. "When?"

"Last night," he gasped as he talked. "By an elf."

Chris and I looked at each other. Then we couldn't help what happened next. We laughed.

"What?" Dirk asked, standing up a little, starting to catch his breath.

"An elf?" Chris laughed. "Are you crazy?"

"It was an elf," he said. "I saw him running away from my house with my scooter in his hand."

"Why would an elf steal your scooter?" I asked.

"Angelo said someone stole his gift too—the high-hat," Dirk said.

Dirk's parents said they didn't touch the scooter. "You know my mom," he said. "She'd give it away to some poor kid who didn't get anything just because she hated that I complained about it." He said Angelo loved his high-hat, he didn't complain a bit. He knew elves took his gift back too. "Those elves must be doing this without Santa even knowing about it," he said, "but why?"

That was about all we could say. What more could we say? Dirk was crazy. But his scooter was gone—he said taken right from under the tree.

That night, I stared at my basketball almost until midnight—just to make sure no elves took it. Then I thought, I know why that elf took Dirk's scooter. He tried to trick Santa. Sure, that must be it. He told Santa he'd be good, but he wasn't. I waited, and no elves came to take my ball. I could see it on the floor as my eyelids got heavier and heavier and until I couldn't see it anymore because I was asleep.

The days passed, and I protected that ball at night. I never let it out of my sight. After a week, I stopped watching it so carefully. I mean I didn't lose it or anything, I just didn't sleep with it in my bed. After a few months, I'd forgotten about Dirk's story.

TWO

Travis Johnson's Testimony,
Part 2 of 8: A New Scheme—Trap an Elf

It was a tough year for me. Like Easter. There I am staring at a basket that I know I've seen before. I mean, year after year the Easter Bunny uses the same basket over and over again? Enough already. Well, I ate too much candy that day and got a toothache. Before you know it, there goes one of my last kid teeth. So I get this dollar bill under my pillow, but this one looked like one my mom gave me a few days before to buy a newspaper. There wasn't one at the store, so I gave it back to her. Now it ends up under my pillow and the tooth is gone.

Soon it was Christmas time again. Dirk and Angelo were still hanging around with Chris and me. I don't know why. Chris and I were playing in the woods near her house. We weren't playing pirates like we had before. I don't know, pirates was getting boring. We weren't looking for chipmunks either. We'd seen enough. She was skimming stones by the creek. That never got old. Dirk and Angelo were supposed to meet up with us and we were going to ride bikes on the trail, but they hadn't gotten there yet.

"My mom says all the ads for Christmas start earlier and earlier," she said.

"Yeah," I said. "Well, that doesn't bother me."

She smiled. "You know, I'm not so sure about Santa," she said.

"What about him?" I asked.

"You know, what the kids in class say," she kicked at the dirt looking for new stones. "I don't say anything, but sometimes I wonder."

"Yeah, but... you got that," I pointed at her pink jacket.

"I know," she said. "But my mom does a lot of shopping. Maybe she just bought it."

She was a little sad, it seemed. I don't like to see her sad, it makes me sad. We both sat quietly for a moment. I wanted to say something, but I couldn't think of anything. Then I just blurted out, "Hey at least you didn't have some elf come and take it away!" We both laughed.

Just then, Dirk showed up. "What's so funny?" he asked.

"Nothing," I said.

"Yeah," he said. "Listen, I've been thinking about that elf again."

Chris said, "Again? He's all you think about. Forget about him."

"I can't," he said. "I've been going over it again and again. Why would an elf take my scooter back?"

"Maybe he's a bad elf, not with Santa at all," I suggested.

"No," Dirk replied. "No because then Santa would know about it and make him stop. No, I think he's working for Santa all right."

"I know why he took your toy," Chris said. "Because you should have been on the list of bad kids and somehow you tricked Santa to be on to the good list."

Dirk thought about that for a moment, like he had never thought of that, then said, "I think Santa's maxed out."

"Maxed out?" I asked.

"Think about it," Dirk said. "He's got all these kids who want toys. That's expensive to make all those toys. So he takes some back."

Chris and I didn't say anything.

"This year, I've got a plan," he said and pointed to me. "We're gonna get Santa and get anything we want for Christmas."

"Wait," I said. "Why me?"

"Because me and Angelo are out," he said. "We got our gifts taken back!"

"Why not me?" Chris asked.

"You'll never do it," Dirk said. "Besides you're a..." he stopped, "a good kid."

"I'm a good kid," I said. "Santa didn't take my present back."

"Exactly," Dirk said. "You can get on his good side. Get another gift, then we set a trap."

"Set a trap?" Chris asked.

"Yeah," Dirk said, "a trap. For the elf who takes the presents back. First, you'll be goodie goodie till Christmas, get the gift. Then afterward you'll do something really bad after you get the gift. Then we set the trap, and we take pictures. We'll send copies to Santa and bribe him. Tell him the elf pictures will be all over the news. What will people think when they find out Santa sends out elves to steal back toys?"

"I don't get it," I said.

Dirk rolled his eyes. "Santa won't want people to know he steals stuff back. He'll give us anything to keep this quiet. Z-Box for you, motor scooter for me. And lots more. To keep us quiet. Get it?"

I looked to Chris then back to Dirk. I said, "Wait we're going to hold an elf hostage so we can get lots of presents from Santa?"

"Exactly," Dirk said and smiled.

"And you wonder why you're not on the good kid list," Chris remarked and started riding away on her bike to the trail.

"I'm not helping with that," I said and joined her.

He ran to keep up with us at first, then we biked faster and lost him. For the next few days, Dirk kept trying to get me to set the trap. He even got Angelo to pressure me. "You've got to do this for the other kids who get their toys taken away," he said. The two of them wouldn't stop. Chris was helping me tell them no, and I needed her help. Then she went away to see her grandparents in Florida. I was alone with those two, and they were bugging me bad.

I got a CD player that year. Big deal. Dirk came to my house the day after Christmas. He said he had the perfect plan. Mrs. Green was an old lady who lived a couple doors down from my apartment. She sat on her front porch most days, cleaning out her garden when it was cold or watering her flowers when it was warm. When we would walk by, she'd always have something to say like, "You better not spit on the sidewalk in front of my house," or "I don't want to ever see you around here pulling up my plants." Dirk would say something like, "Who cares about your stupid plants?" or "How about if I spit on your plants—would that be okay?"

I never knew what to say when Dirk talked mean to her. Part of me wanted to tell him to cut it out. "She's an old lady," I'd think. "She's grouchy I get it, but leave her alone." Part of me wanted to ignore what he was saying because she was so grouchy. That's the part that won all the time.

Dirk said, "Stay right here. I've got a perfect plan."

Angelo and I waited a few minutes until Dirk brought back a big trash bag. By this time, Mrs. Green was inside her house. "You walk this to her porch and dump it!" He said.

"What is it?" I asked.

He made his voice lower and came closer to me to say it, "Leftovers from Christmas dinner."

"Yeah," Angelo said. "That's perfect."

"I'm not doing that," I said. I really wished Chris had been there to stop them from bugging me. She was still in Florida; why did she have to go for so long? They kept telling me I had to do it because if the elves saw them dumping the trash it would be a big deal. They told me I had to do it for the "poor, helpless" kids who get their toys taken away. It was tough to argue with them. I was getting tired of listening to them.

I took the leftovers from Dirk's dinner. It didn't feel that heavy, I thought. My heart was up closer to my throat, I felt it. I slowly walked over to her porch. Dirk and Angelo were talking to me, telling me to move faster. I walked up the steps a little faster, afraid that she might come out any minute. Just that fast, I dumped it all on her front porch— it was disgusting. Turkey bones, mashed potatoes, apple pie. What a mess. All three of us were down the street within seconds. She never came out.

That night, I tossed and turned in my sleep. And when I did finally fall asleep, I had this crazy dream where Santa and the Easter Bunny were both chasing me with bags full of garbage! And I don't even believe in the Easter Bunny— who does, right?

The next day, I saw Mrs. Green on her front porch. She glanced at me as she was rinsing down the rest of what was left on her porch. I thought she was going to say something, but she didn't. I tried not to look back because I was scared of what she might say. Then I found Dirk waiting at my apartment.

"What do you want?" I asked.

"Look at her," he said about Mrs. Green. "We got her good, right?"

"Shut up about her," I said and pushed him away to get into the front door of my apartment complex. "What we did wasn't right."

"Wait," Dirk said as he caught up to me. "This is all about the setup, Travis. We'll make it up to her when we catch that elf. We can even ask Santa to give us presents for her. Like... a... rocking chair or something, right?"

I stood there a moment and thought maybe Dirk could be right.

"She might like socks," I said.

"Right!" He said, "Grandma socks! Whatever. Listen, it's time to set that trap."

"Set it up? Now?" I asked.

"Hey, we're already late," he said. "What if that elf came back to get your CD player last night?"

"I don't care about that CD player," I said. And I didn't care about it. I wanted a Z-Box. I don't even have any CDs. I don't even like music that much. It wasn't tough to give that up.

In my room, Dirk's older brother came over to set up some net trap that he used for catching animals in the woods when he went hunting. Dirk's older brother is like ten years older than us, really old. He's weird too. He has a long beard and wild hair.

"Not sure what you little dudes are doing," he said. "But this trap is spring loaded. Don't step on it yourself, you'll be swinging from the ceiling if you're not careful. Don't put the bait on this metal thing—that's the trigger for the trap. Put it right beyond that trigger. Once the catch is in the net, you got to hold this rope to keep him there."

I didn't know what spring loaded meant, but it sounded dangerous. Right away, I thought of my mom. I didn't want her to come in my room without my knowing about it. I found the key to my bedroom and locked the door from then until we finished with this crazy thing.

Dirk handed me a can.

"What's this?" I asked.

"Pepper spray," he said.

"What's that?" I asked.

"A spray you shoot in somebody's face to make them go blind," he said.

"What?" I said. "I'm not taking this."

"They don't go blind forever, dude," his brother said. "Just for a little bit."

"Yeah," Dirk said. "It's just in case there's more than one."

"More than one what?" I asked.

"Yeah, more than one what?" his brother asked.

"More than one elf," Dirk said.

"Elf? What?" his brother asked as if he couldn't believe what he'd just heard. "You guys are trapping elves?" he laughed and started to walk out. "You all are some nutty little kids."

With his brother gone, Dirk put the pepper spray in my hand. "Look, you don't have to use it. Just threaten him with it."

"Who?" I asked.

"The other elf, if there is another one. I think there is another one," he said. "How else are we going to keep the other elf here if there's another one who can easily get him down from this net? Get it? So call me after you catch the elf. I'll get over here with a camera and we'll get a picture for the newspaper."

"Why don't I just take a picture?" I asked.

"Because you'll be holding the rope to keep the net up and the pepper spray," he said. "Man do I have to teach you everything?"

My mom was working the late shift. When she does, my aunt from across the hall comes over and makes sure I'm safe before she goes to bed. After she left, I positioned myself in my room—just like Dirk said—and waited.

Later that night, I heard footsteps outside on the fire escape. I sat behind my bed watching. I couldn't believe it! Dirk was right! There he was. An elf! Sort of like the ones you see on a TV Christmas special! It was easy for him to get in the window because he was tiny and thin. When he got in, he had to adjust these thick, dark glasses. I never saw an elf wear dark glasses like that before—even on the TV specials! Well, I guess I'd never seen an elf before—ever! So what did I know?

The skinny elf didn't walk around too much. He walked straight up to the CD player. Even in the dark he knew where it was!

And it was right by the trap!

THREE

Editor's Note: The Counsel requested to hear from Honcho next. Honcho read a preface before his testimony (included below).

Well if the kid gets to start from the beginning, I should too. I wrote this journal that I'd like to share with the Counsel as my testimony. It has everything I want to say to the Counsel as well as to parents and older siblings everywhere (in case they ever get to read this). This journal is a testimony for Counsel but a cautionary tale for those caretakers—so I hope they're able to read it too someday. But just to be sure I'm clear—I don't want parents or older siblings reading this to their kids. This isn't some *'Twas the Night before Christmas* feel-good story. So for the Counsel and caretakers everywhere, here it goes.

My name is Honcho, but before you caretakers reading get all sappy on me, like "Oh, look at the cute elf," spare me. Like I said, this is not some little kid's story. In fact, if you got a kid you fawn all over, you'll want to keep this testimony from them and deliver the story—the message—in your own way. You picking up what I'm laying down, friends?

"Oh, I don't fawn all over my child," you say? Spare me that too. I know you do. You lavish them with gifts they mostly don't deserve. You make their lunch till their twenty years old. You let them live in your house till they're thirty. What is wrong with you? But okay, let's just stick with the younger kids, like under ten. They're who this story is supposed to help. That kid who has graduated college and is still chugging milk right from the bottle in your fridge—that mess is all yours to clean up. No, this is about the smaller kids.

"You are one mean elf," you say? Okay I'll wear that hat since it fits. But why don't you wear yours too? That's all I'm saying.

To the caretakers out there, let me give some background. My boss is Big Nick. You know him by many names. I call him Big Nick. Get it? I'm the leader of his elfin elite. He deploys this highly skilled, expertly trained legion *after* Christmas. Our mission is simple: take back the toys from kids who were pretending to be nice. Ah, I feel like some caretaker heads are nodding out there. Good. You're getting it.

"You are being a little gruff, little elf," you sneer. Wake up. I told you: this story is not for kids. Keep it up or I'll throw a foul word in here that you'll definitely have to skip if you're still reading this out loud to your kid. So cut it out.

Like most great armies, my special forces arose at a crossroads in history. It was a time when kids were staring to believe in Big Nick when they were turning nine or even ten. That's way longer than kids believed years ago! Early in my elf career, kids stopped believing in Nick by seven at the latest! "Why is this such a big deal?" you ask. Listen, you know as well as I do that when kids turn ten, it's harder to figure out what they want as a gift. When they're younger, a doll or a baseball. But at ten, they want more—sophisticated electronic equipment, digital gaming, and all that. Who can keep up with that kind of production?

"Why do kids believe in Santa longer?" you ask. It would appear that each staff member of North Pole Industries has a theory. Maybe there are more families with just one kid. They've always been tough, those "only children." No big brothers or sisters to spoil the idea of Santa for them. Sometimes it's parents who can't keep their kids in line so they bring up Santa as a threat. "If you're not good, I'll call Santa," they say. To those parents I say watch that milk in your fridge. Guaranteed your kid is drinking right from the bottle.

There was this one dad I knew who had a phony telephone number on his cell phone that was supposedly for "Santa." It wasn't our number. But he'd dial just to threaten his ten-year-old daughter if she got out of line. Now that is sick. I like how sinister it is, don't get me wrong, but it's sick.

Despite popular belief, Big Nick is actually pleased to see fewer kids believing in him. You could say it's because he wants people to see past all the pageantry of Christmas to understand its deeper meaning—and that is one factor. But the main reason? Economics, baby!

Listen, elves don't work for free. We have to get fed, have proper housing—albeit the houses can be a little smaller than yours. We even want a bump in pay when we take a supervisory job. Who can blame us? Sometimes elves are the worst people to supervise. We can be stubborn, mouthy, and plain belligerent!

Bottom line: Big Nick's got a financial statement to balance like any business owner.

If unwavering belief in Santa was one factor that led to the Repo Elf Squad, the other was N2N Hackers. "What in the world is that?" you ask. These are kids who hack into the Nice list and get themselves off the Naughty list. In short, they fake us out by completely pretending to be nice. They are not only naughty, they're the naughtiest! They're brats who go beyond basic depravity. Listen, we figure most kids will pretty up their case for a toy they really want, right? Sure, they get all sugary sweet and fetch your slippers and pipe (although I may be thinking of a century or two ago with that example). There may be little—well I hate to say lies—exaggerations. But the N2N Hackers? They're different.

Let me explain why.

Before you go thinking an N2N Hacker doesn't believe in Nick, think again. N2N Hackers believe all right, unlike most brats who don't believe but have doting, simple-minded parents who get them all kinds of presents anyway. Strike a little too close to home for you—all that what I just said? You don't think you fawn over your kid, right? So how could I be talking to you? Listen, friend, you're not all that bad. I'm just trying to help you see the light to save you—and your kid. "From what?" You ask. Read on.

Unlike most other naughty kids, N2N Hackers also have unscrupulous ways of making themselves look better for the singular goal: get the gift! Oh, not like there isn't a boatload of kids like this—you know the ones who turn on the charm to get their gift and then after Christmas—bam!—they go back to their old ways. That is just like an N2N Hacker, don't get me wrong, but the Hackers have an especially disgusting way of pouring on the sickly thick, sappy sweetness only to revert to monstrous terrors right after tearing open the gift we send, the very one they requested. Boggles the mind.

Enough about the Hackers. Let me tell you more about my story and how I was chosen to be a Repo Elf.

Not all elves want to work with Big Nick. Does that surprise you? Make your eyebrows raise a little? It's not like the big man has us all under some funky magical spell—like "ooh, Santa, we want to work for you...we want nothing more than to spend every third quarter slaving 24/7 for you."

Many elves don't even take up the work everyone thinks we value so much. I personally ran my own elfin used car lot; excuse me, I mean my own certified pre-owned auto dealership. In fact, every year we held a "How Many Elves Can You Fit in a Hummer" contest. We got as high as twenty to be exact.

But the used car business is not all it's cracked up to be. First, most elves can't reach the pedals. That makes selling a used car to an elf nearly impossible. Then, whatever taller elves remain ultimately cannot understand why the car can't fly. How annoying. I can't tell you how many leases I had to defend in court because the elf insisted that they were told the car could fly.

Then there's the financing. Don't even get me started about the financing. They say they've got the cash, and then they start telling stories each month—like, "oh, one of the reindeer must have eaten my money" or "It's December 26, give an elf a break." It wasn't worth it, so I took the job with Big Nick.

After spending a little time on the front line, Nick saw my potential as a supervisor. I spent years turning around the Electronics Division. Santa's right hand manager is a guy named Charge. He made me the leading manager of two sections, Toy Trains and Remote Control. To say the job was burdensome is an understatement. It was a comedy and tragedy all at once. On one hand, the elf lobby called "Toy Trains Better Wired" and on the other "Set the Trains Free." My job, as always was to keep the two sides on a level playing field. "Don't expect fairness," I'd say to them, "hope for equity instead."

We worked our way to solutions, but it was tedious. I was secretly wishing for a change, a new challenge.

Do you believe in God, reader? "Oh no you didn't just ask that," you say? Okay don't get all squirrelly on me. How about this: do you believe in a universe? "You'd have to condemn Galileo to not believe in a universe," you grumble. Good. Then whether you believe in God or the universe, you believe in timing. Timing. It is the essential element of life that, whether you like it or not, rules us all. Like gravity, timing works invisibly and silently, but it's working all the same. When you admit it and work with it (instead of against it or ignoring it), you live a more fulfilled life. Admit it now or later—or never—makes no difference to me. I'm not your judge. You stopped reading this out loud to your kid now, didn't you? Good, then I can stay away from the foul words.

What happened next was perfect timing, and not just because it advances the story but because it was.

FOUR

I knew something was up when Nick and his right-hand man Charge were the only two in Nick's office waiting to talk with me. Let me tell you a little about Charge. Nick doesn't make a move without him—right-hand guy like I said. That's okay I guess, but I'm not so sure I trust the guy. First off, he puts me in the rotten position of managing that merger—and that was enough to tick me off! But besides that, to have Nick's ear all year long—be that close to everything he says or does. Well, if you subscribe to that basic tenant of business that "absolute power corrupts absolutely" you got to think Charge's privilege goes to his head sometimes. Not to mention, he's not even an elf. That's right. Big Nick decided to get an "outsider's perspective" on the whole problem of kids believing in Santa too late in life. He was recruited under the snowcap. That's what we call anywhere outside the North Pole.

Charge had an under the snowcap name, but none of us knows what it is—except Nick of course. Charge started the conversation that day in Nick's office.

"I's no secret you're not happy with your current job," Charge said to me.

"You're the one who put me there," I said. "But I'll make the best of it. I always do."

"That's why we like you," said Charge, "but we've got another project in mind."

"Oh?" I said.

"You've seen the reports," Charge continued. "More kids are believing in Santa longer. We haven't determined why, but we've got some people working on it. You've undoubtedly heard the theories, the decrease in siblings, parents invoking Santa's good name. Of course, we don't want to disappoint these kids—it's just not in Santa's nature."

Nick added quickly, "Yes but let's face it, this trend has been going on too long—and it's not stopping any time soon. You know we can keep up with demand much longer. We're talking nine- and ten-year-olds. We can't keep up the output. You know that, right?"

I nodded, "I know, Nick. I know."

Charge continued, "One thing that will help—one thing we need to get a handle on right away anyway—is the N2N Hacker epidemic. If we can somehow that gnawing thorn in our side, it would help us keep costs down."

"Makes sense," I said. "What do you have in mind?"

Nick took out a big report and tossed it in front of me.

"Santa's Repo Elves," Charge said.

"Repo Elves," I murmured.

"A special forces unit," Charge said. "Deployed right after Christmas. By then we will have compiled all the worst of the N2N Hackers. They'll be sorted on a precise, confidential itinerary in the most clandestine operation to ever come out of this office since The Stealth Sleigh. The squad will repossess the toys sent to the N2N Hackers. No more letting these kids enjoy the fruits of their wicked labors."

I smiled and stood up and reached out my hand to Charge. He took it. "Gentlemen," I said breaking my grip with Charge and taking Nick's hand, "I'm your man."

The first year of managing my team couldn't have gone any better. First, I was given the authority to handpick my squad. Nick is no dummy. He knows how to empower his managers to let them make their own decisions. There were five of us. I had to pick the kind of elves that are quick, bold—but knew how to keep a secret. This was not a given in the elfin world. After a few hot chocolates, some elves could be persuaded to give up secrets that would send their own mothers to prison!

Next was the training. I set up the objectives and exercises. Elves needed to know the latest technology to remain incognito, identify and lift items—even in dimly lit rooms—and make a flawless escape. We developed a small testing room to play out all sorts of scenarios, from the screaming kid to the screaming parent and everything in between.

Our task was simple. We would enter a home, identify Santa's present, and swiftly snatch it up before anybody knew we were there. It was great to watch the kid the next day. First came the crocodile tears, then the brat takes it out on the parents. "You stole it," would be the first outburst—it was like music to our ears.

Our task could have been a little overwhelming. There were so many kids who deserved to have their toys repossessed. With such a seemingly daunting task, we needed to prioritize the missions. This is where Sequence came in. Sequence is my right-hand elf. He kept us running a right ship. For the list, he calculated a child's chance of reverting back to his or her naughty ways. Perhaps an N2N Hacker would pleasantly greet relatives on Thanksgiving but then swiftly kick the same guests in the shins by the New Year's Eve party. This type of turnaround was formulated into an equation whereby Sequence could analyze which kids were more important to hit—first by degree of naughtiness then by geographic region. If someone was marked a priority five that meant if we didn't get to him or her that was okay. After all, every N2N Hacker was never allowed on the Nice List again. So if we didn't get their toy back, it was the last toy they'd ever get form us anyway.

Let me explain. The kid who kicked guest at the New Year's Eve party, believe it or not, was probably a priority five. Hey, what can we say? There are a lot of brats out there, we only had to go after the worst of them. Now, there was this one kid who got together with some friends and threw eggs at cars on Christmas night. Definitely a priority one. And that kid hated the toy he received, which is why the eggs got tossed. Hating the toy you got—and doing something nasty because of it—definitely moves you up on the priority list!

Case #4368: Dirk and the Scooter: This report is really about one particular N2N Hacker gang. These kids were a band of trouble. Dirk was the leader, and he was the first to get his gift repossessed. He was the only kid ever to be an N2N Hacker twice. The first time Dirk was on the N2N Hacker list, Sequence hadn't tabulated all his data and the kid was a priority five. I don't blame him—it was a busy year. We didn't repossess Dirk's toy that year. Somehow, and I can't tell you exactly how, he got on the Nice List again. He was rude to his mother right on Christmas morning, complaining that the game we'd left him wasn't computerized. Little brat.

This following year, we were ready for Dirk. The kid was priority number one. We approached his house through the woods in the backyard. The windows were dark except for the kitchen, but it seemed nobody was there. Sequence brought out the schematic for the house. "Upstairs bedroom, above the kitchen," he said. I pointed toward the kitchen then up.

"Maybe that one," I said.

Sequence mumbled, "Chimney is here, down to the living room, over to the stairs here."

I hate to say it, but Big Nick's got it easy. One flash and he's down the chimney, puts the toys under the tree, and poof he's gone. We had to go about things much differently. We can't magically transport like the big man. But we are smaller, we got that going for us. But that gift is far, far away from the tree—and that tree may not even be up. We slide down the chimneys like ninjas. From there we got to find that toy! Most times it's in the bedroom. But it may be under the tree (if we're that lucky) or in a toy box down the basement or in a special toy room. We never knew going in. We had to do the best we could to find that toy.

By our second year, we had better way to identify the toys. We would paint a stripe in an infra-red solution then we wore special goggles in the dark to spot it. Much better method than the old way with flashlights. We would definitely get spotted more often with the lights.

Oh, and the dogs. We always needed to have intelligence on dogs. They were the worst. Growling would be okay, but when they went into all-out barking that was the end. Cats were a little better, but not by much. If you stepped on a tail that was it—your cover was blown.

We arrived at the kid's house. No pets on our report. Sequence and I would have to sneak in and start poking around. We were looking for a scooter we left him that year. Scooters are sometimes easy to get back, when they're left outside or in an open garage. But we didn't see it at all outside. With any luck, the kid was ticked off and left it under the tree. It's easiest to find there. I begged Sequence to wait for the kid to take the scooter outside. It was so much easier to pull the toy from outside.

"We've been on this stake out for days," he said to me. "And I've been waiting to get this kid for a year now. We don't have much time. We'll be pulled from the project. This may be the last night to get it."

We reviewed the plans. If something happens that surprises us, there is a side door near the kitchen that would provide quick escape. We would not be able to get back up the chimney if we're caught in the act. We made our way down the chimney. It was a slow descend, creeping long quietly. With any luck, the scooter will be right under the tree. If he took it to his room, it would mean more sneaking through the house.

Sequence peeked from the chimney into the living room.

"Tree is still up," he said looking through the goggles. "And there it is right under that tree," he said and took the goggles away to look at me. "Still has the bow on it," he handed me the goggles. "I can get this myself," he said and slid down the remainder of the chimney and crawled into the living room. I crawled down and joined him in the room in case there was a surprise dog or anything to mess this up. We would escape together through that side door if necessary.

He tip-toed behind a sofa, keeping his focus on the prize. Suddenly, a light turned on in the hallway.

"Forget it," I whispered as loud as I could. "Someone's coming. Pull back, soldier!"

"No way," Sequence said. "I've waited too long to get this gift back from this Hacker." I could hear feet shuffling down the hallway steps. Sequence grabbed the scooter and ran toward the opposite side hallway toward the side door. I've never seen him fly like that—he looked like one of the reindeer. I followed right behind as a light came on. I'm not sure if Dirk could see us. We opened the side door and lunged out of the house, across the yard, and into some bushes nearby. The kid came to the side door really fast. We could hear him yell as he ran back into the house, screaming for his mommy with his little black spiked hair and big crybaby eyes!

"That was close," Sequence said, out of breath.

"That punk?" I replied. "He's no taller than you, and no skinnier than me. We could have taken him." It was true. The kid was the shortest of his bunch of friends. I gathered up our things and indicated we should get out of there. "Well," I said, "I don't want to get found out by some brat like that. Let's go."

"Yeah," Sequence replied. "We got the gift back anyway!"

Just then, the kid came back out with a flashlight! He went in the other direction so we took off as quickly as possible. He heard us, but by then we had gotten a pretty good lead. We went down a side street then into an alley. He kept going past the alley. We stayed there for a few minutes. We heard his mother calling on him, and he slowly slinked back toward the house—flashlight off.

After the adventure that night at Dirk's house, we tracked down a friend of his, Angelo, to make sure he didn't get a chance to get on the Nice List either. We waited outside to spy on the skinny little runt with his big fat curly hair as he searched and searched for that high-hat cymbal.

"I'm surprised he's not looking through his mop of a head for that high-hat," I said and Sequence snickered. We were watching him from outside his bedroom window.

"He's got a lot of hair, that little dude," he said.

"C'mon, let's get out of here," I said. We were too busy to get a detailed report on the third kid in their gang, Travis, that year. He wasn't on the N2N Hacker list.

Case #4401: Travis and the CD Player: The following year was our third season working with this particular bunch of brats! Sure enough we caught Travis, a day or so after Christmas, throwing the leftovers from Christmas dinner all over the front porch of an old lady from their neighborhood. I have to say, this was somewhat of a surprise. I mean—the kid didn't look all that bad with his friendly smile. Guess you can't judge a book by its cover, huh?

Travis wanted a Z-Box that year, only the most coveted electronics toy a kid could want. But even Santa had the insight, and some elfin reports, to know what the kid deserved at best was a CD player. I was glad to see the CD player was still in production. After all, I had written the report "MP3: No Challenge to the Pre-Teen CD Player." The report emphasized that kids in that age group were not ready to start downloading tunes and still needed to have a player.

Sequence reviewed the schematic for the layout of the kid's apartment. It was easy to see that the best way to his room was from the fire escape outside his bedroom window. We climbed up and looked into his window. The CD player was right in his bedroom, we could see it with the goggles. The window was already partly open. It seemed strange the window was open for such a cold night, but we didn't mind having easier access.

"I'll handle this one," Sequence said. "I've been waiting to repo this kid's gift since he dumped garbage on that nice lady's front porch." He tiptoed across the floor to the gift. He was doing everything right, slithering up to the gift with one foot already out the door. He reached for the CD player, and then I heard it out of nowhere.

FWIP!

FIVE

What happened next was nuts! All of a sudden the elf was hanging from the ceiling all tangled up in the rope net thing Dirk's brother laid out. I was holding on to the rope on the other side with the spray in my pocket. Good thing mom was working late. She would have definitely heard all the noise. Holding the rope, I reached out and turned on the light. Just then, another elf came in the window. It was Honcho. At first, I remember thinking, *this is not your average elf!*

"What are you doing here?" he asked.

"What are *you* doing here?" I asked. "You're the one who's in my room!"

"What's this?" he asked pointing at the rope.

"It's a trap," I said.

"Well get him down," he said. "You don't know who you're messing with!

Honcho started coming at me. I took the spray from my pocket and pointed it at him. "Hey," I said, "get away!"

"What's that," he asked.

I couldn't think so I just said, "P-p-peppermint spray!"

"Man, you are some kind of punk kid, aren't you? Threatening me with pepper spray! Trapping my best elf."

"Oh yeah...well...what kind of elf are you?" I asked. "Taking back a kid's gifts!"

"Oh, you're one to talk," Honcho said. "Leaving a bunch of trash on that poor old lady's front step."

We both didn't say a word.

"Okay party's over," the elf said. "Let him down."

"He's not going anywhere," I said. "Not until I talk to Santa."

"You?" Honcho said and laughed. "You talk to Santa. Okay, let him down and maybe we'll let you keep the CD player." He started walking toward me.

I held up the spray, and he backed up. "I didn't ask for that CD player," I said. "I wanted a Z-Box."

"You don't deserve a Z-Box," he said, "after what you did to that little old lady." He stood quietly for a moment. "So what do you want, kid, huh? A Z-Box?"

"I want a thousand Z-Boxes..." I said.

"A thousand?" he asked and laughed.

And what I said next I don't know where that came from. I never thought about it, but it just came out. "I want to sell them to help my mom. She works seven days a week since my dad died."

The elf stood quietly for a moment. He looked like he didn't hear me. "What?" he asked. He talked more quietly. "Kid, what do you want?"

"A thousand Z-Boxes," I said again.

"Kid, we can't give you that. I'm sorry," he said. He was really quiet now.

"Then we start taking pictures and calling newspapers," I said. I didn't quite figure out the rest so easily. I took the rope and tied it around my closet doorknob. It seemed to be holding. Spray pointed at Honcho, I walked to the cordless phone near me and dialed Dirk to tell him and hung up the phone. "Listen, my friend is coming over to take pictures. Soon, everyone will know about Santa's elves who steal toys back." I got on the phone again. "Chris? Finally you're home. Get over here right away. You're not going to believe this." I hung up the phone again.

Honcho looked at me for a moment. He took out his cell phone. He punched in one number so I knew it was speed dial! Must have been Santa. He talked into the phone. "Miss Keeper? Yeah it's me Honcho. Can you get Charge on the phone?"

Honcho stood there for a moment waiting. "Your friend's coming over, huh?" he said, "Who's that? Dirk? Let me tell you something, kid. Dirk is no friend of yours. He's doing nothing but dragging you down! And you're not talking to Santa. The best you'll get is someone from his staff—if you're lucky!" Then he got back on the phone.

"Charge, yeah it's me Honcho. We got kind of a situation here."

SIX

Nick's Testimony,
Part 1 of 1: Taking Action under the Snowcap

The sleigh bells jingled on the door of my office. Charge entered, and he didn't look good. His eyes were bloodshot, his face looked pale and long. The little vein that normally stays dormant on his forehead was protruding. He'd been yelling at someone. But probably the thing that tipped me off that something was really wrong is that my wife was with him.

"Oh my," I said and smiled. "You two only come in together when something is really wrong. Barbie doll elves threatening to strike again? We can't give in to their demands: no real hair for Ken."

"This is serious, dear," my wife said.

"There is a kid under the snowcap," Charge said. "He's captured Sequence."

"Sequence," I said. "What do you mean he's captured Sequence?"

"He trapped Sequence," Charge continued. "He has him in a net dangling from his bedroom ceiling. He's holding Honcho off with a can of pepper spray. Kid laid the trap for us while we were trying to get back the gift we sent him this year."

"How could this happen?" I asked.

"We touched on this in our preliminary reports years back," Charge explained. "I mean we sort of discounted the idea that any kid was smart enough or strong enough to capture an elf, let alone keep him hostage."

"We were obviously wrong," I said, mostly to myself. "So what does he want?"

"A thousand Z-Boxes," my wife said.

Laughing a little, I twirled my whiskers. This is something I don't normally do except under stress or when I think a customer—oh, I mean a wee tot—is watching me from afar as I'm doing my job. "He's kidding right?" I looked over to the production floor, which was quiet now after the holiday. "It takes a lot of magic out of me to keep up with the crazy production cycle we just finished—let alone to fulfill this insane request." I circled my desk and made a drink. Eggnog with an extra sprinkling of nutmeg.

"Oh honey," my wife said, "do you really need that?"

"Believe me, I do," I said and gulped.

"Well, fix me one, will you dear?" she said and smiled.

Chuckling, I poured another glass. "You, Charge?" I asked.

"Not for me," he said. Then he told me he assembled this very panel of Regional Vice Presidents in this very board room, as you all will recall.

You want my honest reaction? I'm under oath, right?

I asked, "And why would you do that?"

He said, "Come on, Nick."

My wife said, "Remember what we say to our managers. Get your whole team in on the decision-making process."

So I shrugged, gulped the last of my drink, and said, "Fine, I'll talk with them." Then I turned to Charge and said, "You get down there and talk to this kid. Get there as fast as you can."

Can I tell you all something, members of the Counsel? I love you guys, I really do. You represent the essence of holiday generosity throughout the world—in every continent, in every country. I'm glad you are asking for this inquiry, and my being here supports it. That night, when everything was a mess under the snowcap, I remember walking up to this board room—with Mrs. Claus— standing outside that door. You were all in here talking and joking around.

"Listen to them," I said. "Was I ever that bad?"

She said, "You were worse. More jolly than all of them put together."

"What happened?" I asked.

She put her arms around me and kissed my forehead. "You've been at this for hundreds of years, sweetheart."

I knew what she was talking about, but who else would do this job? When the door opened and we walked in, you all got quiet. Because nobody else was there except for us, and because it should be part of the permanent record, let me recount my experience that night—and you all can agree or not to my account.

Chris K., the North American Santa VP, was the first to speak. "What's this we hear about one of our elves being held hostage?"

"How is that possible?" asked Kristof, the European Santa VP, and the oldest member of the group.

"Yes, it was one of the elves," I confessed. "He was in the process of repossessing one of naughty kid's gifts."

"We did not even know there was such a practice until Charge told us minutes ago, sir," said Niko, the Pacific Rim Santa VP. "I mean—that program—it just doesn't seem to be the spirit of what we do here."

I said the same statement then that I make now, gentlemen, "Somebody needs to make the tough decisions around here. You all sit around here with your red noses, your rosy cheeks, yucking it up. You're not the ones who put it on the line, zapping your strength and magical powers every day to make all this happen."

Do you remember what you said, Crikey Cringle, for the record the New Zealand/Australian VP Santa? Do you remember?

"Excuse me, sir," you said. "The one who gives you the power? Does he want to see you taking back toys?"

I didn't have an answer back then, but I have one now. Obviously that answer is no.

The phone rang at that time, as you all may remember. It was Charge, and I had to take it. Travis was holding Sequence hostage, and he called another friend, Dirk. It was no surprise Dirk was in on this whole scheme. It didn't surprise me to find later he was behind it all. I remembered Dirk as the only kid who ever was on the N2N Hacker list twice. Dirk was planning to bring the press into all this and take pictures—expose the whole operation. I had to get down there.

Thankfully it had been a few days after Christmas, so I was starting to get my energy and magic back, as did the reindeer. We flew at the speed of light, getting to the apartment in time—that is before Dirk entered the room.

"Come on, Travis," Dirk said. "Open the door."

"Travis," I called out gently and smiled from the window.

"Santa," he said as my frame pushed through the window. "It's really you."

"It's me."

"I've always believed in you, Santa," he smiled. "I still do."

"That's the problem," Honcho murmured.

"Good to see you, sir," Sequence said to me. I chuckled at the sight of him up in that net.

"Is that Santa?" Dirk asked from the other side of the door. "Travis, open this door!"

"Hang in there, Sequence," I said and laughed. "Well, no pun intended, son!" Turning to Travis, I asked, "All right, my boy, what's going on here?"

Travis stopped smiling, "I just want a Z-Box."

"One Z-Box?" I asked, raising my eyebrows.

"No," Charge said, "a lot more."

"He wants a thousand Z-Boxes," Honcho sneered.

Dirk called from out in the hallway. "Travis, open the door. Come on. I got the newspaper guy here. We'll blow this thing wide open."

"What newspaper?" I called out from inside the room.

There was a pause. *"New York Times,"* Dirk said eventually.

"No way," I said. "Dirk Hendrick you are in enough trouble already. What newspaper?"

Another pause. "All right," Dirk finally said, *"The Online Gazette News Weekly."*

A second voice called out, "We're the twentieth most widely read independent online weekly news service in the tri-state area."

"You're not helping, man," we could hear Dirk whisper on the other side of the door.

I sighed and said, "All right, enough of this." Tipping my eyeglasses down past the bridge of my nose and twirling my whiskers, I touched my nose twice and waved my hand. With a whirlwind of snowflakes, I magically sent Sequence, Charge, and Honcho out of the room and down the street. It was just Travis and me—oh and his CD player.

A third voice came from outside the door. It was a girl's voice. "What's going on in there?" she asked.

Travis stood motionless for a moment, not sure about what just happened. "How did you do that," he eventually asked.

Dirk punched the door, saying, "Who called her? Travis, I know Santa's in there. I'm going to knock the door down."

"How do I do anything," I said.

"Who's in there," the female voice said.

"That's Chris," he said eventually. "Can I let her in?"

"No," I said. "But I want to help you, Travis. Because I like you, and maybe we were all wrong about you. I'm going to give you the most special gift a person can give to another person."

"What's that?" Travis asked.

"A second chance," I said.

"What's that?" he asked. "What do you mean?"

"You'll know," I said.

"But I don't know," he said. "I don't know what that means."

"So take some time to pray about it."

"Pray?" Travis asked. "To who? To you?"

"No," I chuckled. "This is all about Christmas, right?"

"Yeah," he said.

"You're a smart kid," I said as gold snowflakes began to swirl around me. "You'll figure it out."

Within moments, I was gone.

SEVEN

Seeing Santa was enough to make me like a zombie—seeing all that magic made me not able to move. I stood there for a moment, and Dirk was banging at the door. But it was Chris' voice that woke me up. I unlocked the door and Dirk and Chris and the reporter guy came into my room. Dirk was really angry. He walked around my room, looked at the empty net from the trap then out my window.

"What happened?" he asked me. "What took you so long to open the door? Where is he?"

"Who?" I asked.

"*Who*?" Dirk said. He was getting angrier. "Santa, the elf, everyone who was here. I heard voices."

"I heard voices too, Travis," Chris said. "Who was that?"

"It was Santa, and two elves, and another guy," I said. "They were here then poof they were all gone."

"What?" Dirk shouted. "You let them go?"

The reporter looked around. He said, "I thought I'd at least have a human interest story here. You're all a bunch of whackos. I'm out of here." And with that he left.

Dirk walked right up to me and said, "You made a deal with him, didn't you?"

"What?" I asked, still a little bit dizzy from everything that happened. But Dirk's face right up in mine was clearing my head. In fact, his getting right up in my face was making my head fill with fire, it felt like.

"Yeah," Dirk said and pushed me a little, "you made a deal with Santa behind my back."

For the first time, I pushed Dirk back a little, "No," I said. "He just said, 'Enough of this,' and waved his hand, and it was all over. Just like that."

"I don't believe you," Dirk said.

"Fine," I said. "Don't believe me. It's what happened though."

"Wait," Chris said. "Who was here?"

"Santa," I said and was excited to tell Chris. "I had an elf trapped in this net that Dirk's brother set up. He was a skinny elf, and his name was Sequence. And there was a second elf too. His name is Honcho. Then some other guy shows up, a regular person-like guy. Then Santa. It was unbelievable. Then Santa waves his hand like this," I showed her, "and they're all gone." I didn't want to let Dirk know about the "second chance" Santa was giving me. First because I still didn't understand what it meant and second because I didn't want to give Dirk any reason to think I made a deal like he said.

Dirk got right up into my face now. "You're dead," he said to me.

Chris pushed Dirk. "Get out of here, Dirk," she said.

He brushed by Chris to leave the room.

"What was this all about?" Chris asked picking up the net. "You had Santa in this?"

"No, no. There was an elf in there," I said. "Dirk... Dirk..." it was still a little hard to talk about it. And it was embarrassing what had happened. "It started with Dirk pressuring me. He was pressuring me to do something nasty after Santa gave me that CD player for Christmas. He had this idea to dump a bunch of trash on Mrs. Green's front porch—you know the old lady down the street with all the flowers on her porch. You were in Florida, but if you were here you could have helped me fight him and Angelo off."

"Why can't you just tell them no," she said. "So what did Santa look like?"

"Just like you think he would," I said. "Fat, jolly, long beard, long coat! He was amazing. His eyes were... were..."

"Were what?" she asked.

"Magical—but tired," I said. "Hard to explain."

"What did he say to you?" she asked.

"He said he'd give me a second chance," I said. "I told him I didn't know what that means."

"It means he wants to forgive you," Chris said. "But you have to do something to prove you're sorry."

"Forgive me for doing what?" I asked. "It was Dirk's idea to put the trash on Mrs. Green's porch."

"Yeah," she said. "But you're the one who dumped it there, right?" I didn't say anything. "Look, I've got to get home. Tomorrow is our last day on Christmas break, and I want to do something fun. But you think about it, Travis Johnson. I can't believe what you did to poor Mrs. Green. You think about it."

I didn't like what Chris was saying. It was all Dirk's idea, I felt like saying. But I'd already said that a couple of times. So I didn't say anything. I just felt heavy in my heart. What did that feeling mean? Chris left, and I laid down on my bed and slept a little. Soon, my mom was home. She came to my room.

"Honey," she said waking me up, "what's all this rope."

"It's a trap," I said, a little groggy from sleeping. "Dirk's brother brought it over."

"Why?" she asked and snickered.

"It's a long story, mom," I said as she snuggled me in her arms. It was so warm there, so comfortable against her scrubs—even though they smelled like the hospital she worked at.

"I don't know about that Dirk," she said.

"He's a jerk," I murmured, almost falling asleep again. "Dirk the jerk," I said and chuckled.

"What happened here?" she asked.

"I did something wrong I think," I said.

She rocked me and held me closer and was quiet for a little bit. "We'll talk about it later," she said. "We all make mistakes, it's as steady as a second hand."

"What's that mean?" I asked, snuggling closer to her. "Steady as a second hand."

"Your father used to say that," she told me. "You know he fixed watches and clocks—that was his job."

I did know that. She showed me where his shop was in the neighborhood. As she spoke, I remembered dad in his shop when I was a lot younger. He would lean over a wristwatch or a clock using a tiny screwdriver. He would smile at me, and I knew he loved his job. He had other things for sale in the store too—he would always say those things really made him more money. But he loved fixing watches and clocks. Then he got sick, and he couldn't keep the shop any more. Now it's a place where women get their nails done—as if there weren't already five places like that in our neighborhood.

Mom continued to hold me for a while. She said, "It means you can count on something. You can count on the fact you're not alone—every person makes mistakes. Probably they made the very mistake you made. They say a broken clock is right twice a day, but even a clock that's not working has a second hand that's right like 14,000 times throughout the day. That's what your dad said. And he knew. Anyway, it means don't get upset when you make a mistake. Instead stay calm and own up to it. You'll get closer to a solution that way, closer to God too." We sat and snuggled. I could hear traffic sounds outside, which I have always liked. "We all make mistakes," she said again stroking my head—that always felt so good. "But the biggest mistake of all is not owning up to it."

That was the last thing I heard before falling asleep.

EIGHT

Before that night in Travis' room, I'd never been picked up by Big Nick's pixie dust magic show. As head of the Repo Squad, I've been in some binds before, but nothing like this! What a ride! Charge, Sequence, and I were all whisked outside by Big Nick's magic. We were down the block from the kid's house, so much as I could figure out. I mean, the big man could have sent us all right back to the North Pole if he wanted. His power has that much kick— believe it! But I guess being so close after Christmas, he must have been saving up his energy. At least that's what I thought.

"What do you make of all that?" Charge asked in his pretentious way as he dusted himself off.

"All what?" I barked back as I helped Sequence to his feet. "We've been put out. The big man's done it before."

"But why isn't he here?" Charge asked.

"None of our business," I snapped. "What do you think—you get to know why your boss does everything?"

"Listen, Honcho," he began and I could feel my head start to burn, "if it wasn't for you—your error of judgement—Travis would have been taken off the Nice list years ago."

"What are you trying to say, Charge?" I asked. "It's my fault that one kid's slipped through the cracks?"

"Who is in command here," Charge was getting louder and pointing his finger dangerously close to my face.

"Enough!" Sequence called out. "It's my fault. I fell for the trap. So stop fighting."

Charge walked to Sequence and put his arm around him. "No, you couldn't have known there would be a trap. Who could have?"

"Yeah," I said.

"Except maybe your commanding officer," Charge fired back. "It's his job to watch your back."

"Why you overgrown windbag!" I couldn't stop myself. This guy has had it coming a long time—and I've been sizing him up. Sure, he's not an elf, but it's not like I couldn't bring him down easily enough. I jumped on his back and threw him down to the ground.

"You think you're so big, little man," Charge said. "You're nothing but a..."

Just then, a swirl of gold snowflakes appeared on the street. I could feel Big Nick's hand reach out to me and pick me up off of Charge.

"What are you doing?" he asked. "Do you two realize how much trouble you've already caused? I've got kids kidnapping elves, news reporters asking questions. What a mess. Now this?"

"He started it," I said and pointed to Charge.

"Honcho, you sound like those kids back there!" Nick said. "He started it, indeed." He pushed us completely apart. "Sequence, you're coming with me," he said. "You've been through enough today."

"What about us?" Charge asked.

"You're staying here to keep an eye on that kid," he said. "I want reports every day. I'm giving him a second chance."

"Second chance?" I asked. "Why?"

"So we can get a second chance too," he said.

"Wait," Charge said. "How can we report back when we don't know what's going on?"

Nick gave Charge the Mantle of Invisibility, handed down over the centuries. I've only seen it once before so I knew what it looked like. It isn't invisible...like glass. It has a shimmer to it, but when stretched out over someone or something, you couldn't see that shimmer or the thing it was on. You saw nothing. I'm aware that Counsel is familiar with the mantle, but for anyone else reading this testimony, I thought I'd provide background. With that, Nick went back to the North Pole.

With that, we went back to the kid's apartment. When we got there, he was sound asleep. His mom walked in and looked around.

"Honey," she said waking him up, "what's all this rope."

He was a little sleeping, but mustered the strength to say, "It's a trap. Dirk's brother brought it over."

"Why?" she asked and snickered.

"It's a long story, mom," he snuggled up to her and I turned to Charge, who was looking sad but stern at the same time.

"I don't know about that Dirk," she said.

"He's a jerk," the kid nearly whispered in his sleep. "Dirk the jerk," he said. I chuckled, and Charge slapped me, whispering that we may not be visible but we can still be heard.

"What happened here?" she asked.

"I did something wrong, I think," he said.

She held her son closer and rocked gently. "Well, we'll talk about it later," she said. "We all make mistakes, steady as a second hand. But the biggest mistake of all is not owning up to it."

She cuddled for a moment longer and left him to sleep.

We walked down the fire escape to the sidewalk.

"Steady as a second hand," Charge murmured to himself. "Interesting."

"Yeah," I said, "if you know what it means. Come on, get Nick on the phone. Tell him everything's okay and let's get out of here."

Charge called Nick. "Nick, it's me. Listen, everything is fine here. No reporters, no problems. The kid is upstairs in his bed, feeling sorry. He's thinking about your second chance speech." He paused, then said, "Oh, no not speech. No your second chance thing, thingy—oh just the second chance. Yes, thinking about the second chance. Everything worked out great here." I've never seen Charge become even a little rattled or unraveled, and he was sort of doing both. "Okay, well we can stay," he looked at me and I waved frantically to say "no." He continued, "But we don't have anywhere to stay." He listened for a little more, then reached into the Mantle of Invisibility to pull out a credit card. "Got it. Well, don't leave North Pole without it, eh? Okay, we'll talk with you soon." He hung up.

"Can we go back?" I asked.

"We have to stay the night so we can check on the kid in the morning," Charge said.

"Why? Why? Why?" I asked.

"Look, you're as happy about this as I am," Charge said sternly. "Let's go."

We took the Mantle off and began walking around the city. This was not the North Pole, you could tell. Here everything is so gray and brown. Streets, buildings, busses, cars. Nothing bright or cheery for the most part. We rounded a few corners.

"I'm not looking to walk a marathon here, buddy," I said to Charge.

"I know the perfect place to stay the night," he said.

We descended into the ground. It was a little scary and a lot smelly. I said, "Are we sleeping in a cave?"

"Settle down," he said. "We're taking a subway."

"Great," I said. "What's a subway?"

"It's a train that runs underground," he said.

"Do I have to hold my breath," I said.

"It's not under water, just under ground," he said and chuckled. He was so smug.

All the trains I'd ever known ran on top of the ground. This was a new—and frankly silly—concept for me. Why run trains underground? It's better to run them where everyone can see each other and wave at each other. And it was scary down there. It was all dark on the train with lights just whizzing by once in a while. The people on the train did not look happy. Maybe that's because they weren't above ground like they should be! Maybe then they'd smile. A few of them looked at me and smiled, I guess. Some of them looked at me and sneered too though.

We climbed from the underground train and the town looked way different. It was brighter, lots of signs—it was a little more like the North Pole but not really. It still had a creepiness about it. I know it was nighttime but even with all those lights it still seemed too dark. I think I know what it was. There were no lights in the sky that we get to see here. Those lights in the sky, and ours down below, they are in harmony. They don't fight for your attention.

Finally, we rounded a corner and there it was. A big hotel—bigger than I've ever seen at home. Wow, what an impressive place! Charge knew it from when he was living under the snowcap. It was beautiful—five stars, Charge said. I had no idea what that meant, but I wasn't going to let Mr. Smug know that.

"Do you know what 'five stars' means?" he asked me.

"Sure," I said. "It means five stars."

"It means luxury at its best," he puffed. "I used to stay at places like this all the time when I worked down here—and this place often. There are a lot of decisions a person in my spot has to make on a daily basis—decisions that can change many lives. But it comes with its perks."

"Heavy is the head that wears the crown, chump," I said.

"What's that, Honcho?" he asked. "Got something you wanted to say?"

"If you liked it so much, why did you come to the North Pole?" I asked. "We got no hotels up there like this?"

"Working with Santa," he said, "that's like having a five-star life, my friend. That much you should know."

He was right, and I was quiet the rest of the walk. All this grabbing back toys, all of the mergers to manage before that—it all left me longing for a simpler time. We walked into the hotel. I'd never seen anything like this in my life. The ceilings looked like they never ended. There were huge, thick columns chiseled out of beautiful stone, marble floors, people in long overcoats and hats to open doors and just say hello. We walked up to the front desk, and I could barely see the top of the counter, let alone the person behind the counter.

"Yes, I need two rooms, please," Charge said.

"I'm so sorry, sir," said the woman I couldn't see. "We are completely booked up for tonight." She looked down toward me. I smiled at her as best I could, to not look too suspicious. She frowned a little. I didn't know what that meant.

"Oh, well, sorry to hear that," Charge continued. "Any other places to stay around here?"

"I'm sorry," she answered. "But there's a big convention in town. I'm afraid we don't even know where to suggest." Just then her phone rang, and I tugged on Charge's coat. He leaned over.

"What are we going to do now?" I asked.

"I don't know," he said, "but if Santa wanted us to stay overnight, we've got to trust there will not be a problem. Remember, he sees you when you're sleeping, he knows when you're awake... And when you're with Santa, you not only get your solution to a problem, you get better than that."

"I get it," I said. "I get it."

The woman at the counter hung up. "Sir, we just had a cancellation. Would you like that room?"

He stood up right away and said, "Absolutely." He turned to me as if to say, "I told you so." Then, of course, because he is Charge, he actually had to say, "I told you so."

"It's a suite," said the woman, "but we will give you the regular room rate."

"Lovely," Charge said. He turned to me again. Before he had the chance to say it, I stomped on his foot. Watching him try to keep a straight face while paying, knowing he had to have some pain in that foot—well, that was priceless!

The ride on the elevator up was quiet. Charge was trying to look like my stomp on his big foot didn't hurt. The elevator opened and he took the key out. The sign outside our door said "Suite 101." When we walked into the place, I was really impressed. Naturally I selected my bed right away and began bouncing on it. "Wow!" I said. "You can fit my whole family up here."

"I'm sure you could," Charge murmured and began settling into his bed. "Well, let's get some sleep," he said. "We can finish our work by tomorrow with any luck and get out of here."

"But I'm hungry," I said.

"Hungry?" he asked. "You're joking, right?"

"Come on, you got the big man's plastic," I said. "Let's do room service."

"Let's do..." he said and paused a moment, "room service." He snickered. "How do you even know about room service, let alone how to 'do' it. When have you ever had room service? Indeed, when have you ever had a room to which you would have had the opportunity to get... service? Is this not your first night away from the North Pole?"

"For your information," I said, "I was a pre-owned vehicle sales professional, you know. We did have a convention."

"Ooooh," he said, and I braced myself for the insults that would likely follow. "A used car salesman," he said. "And the dealers on the snowcap—all three of you—had a convention. Lovely. And where was that, on the east side of the North Pole?"

"There are five of us," I said. "And I stayed with my cousin, Poncho."

"Honcho and Poncho," he said. "Cute."

I jumped on top of him and twisted his tie. "Listen, chump, if I don't get fed soon," I said, "I'm not going to be nearly as cute! So break out the big man's plastic and let's eat!"

He swatted me away. "Get off the tie, little man," he said. "I can just as easily flush you down the toilet as throw you out that window."

He got up, and I went to the bathroom to wash up. When I got back he was on the phone.

"Get me the nachos," I whispered.

He rolled his eyes. "Do you have nachos?" he asked into the phone. "Yes, one." He turned to me and asked, "What do you want to drink?"

For a moment, I thought then said, "What do they…"

Before I could answer, he said into the phone, "A hot chocolate," and hung up.

"What if I don't like hot chocolate?" I asked.

"Which one of you elves doesn't like hot chocolate?" he asked. "Hmm? It's all you all ever drink!"

"Maybe I'm not like other elves."

"An understatement," he said.

Later, as we were eating our food, Charge looked up from his meal and said, "About tonight's outburst—on the street outside the kid's apartment. I'm sorry. I didn't mean to go off. I was just upset. I personally selected you to lead the Repo Elves, and I stand by that decision. You're a good man."

I nearly choked on my nachos. I said, "You recommended me."

"No," he said. "I selected you. You were my first choice."

"Oh," I said.

"So I hope you can forgive my outburst," he said. "Maybe you can give me a second chance."

"I don't think I ever gave you a first chance," I said and he smiled. "But yeah, Charge. I can give you a second chance. And I hope you can give me one too."

"What?" he asked returning to his food. "Why?"

"For tonight," I said. "Guess I goofed things up."

"Tonight, that was a fluke," he said. "What did his mother say? Steady as a second hand."

"Yeah," I said. "A fluke."

"There may be something wrong with this whole picture," Charge added. "The whole repo elf program that none of us saw. Maybe we all need that second chance."

"All of us?" I asked.

"Yes," he said. "Every single one of us."

NINE

The next morning, after Santa visited me, I woke up to a knock at my door. It was my mom. She said Chris was over. I looked at my watch, it was nearly ten o'clock. I fell out of my bed and into the living room.

"C'mon, it's the last day of Christmas vacation," Chris said. "I've got something perfect to do."

"Oh," I said, rubbing my eyes. "Like sleep?"

"Travis, you better get dressed and go do something today," my mom said. "It's a nice day outside."

"Okay," I said and went back to my room to get changed. Within minutes we were out on the street.

"So what are we doing?" I asked.

We stopped in front of Mrs. Green's house. "Getting your second chance," Chris said. I looked over her shoulder.

"Oh, no," I said. "I'm not going up there."

"Travis," she said, "you have to. What you did was awful."

"She hates me, that lady," I said. "You should have seen the way she looked at me the other day. She was nasty."

Chris just looked at me. Sometimes she looked at me like that, when she knew she was right. And I knew she was too. I couldn't look right in her eyes when she did that. I put my hand over my eyes.

"I'm not looking at you right now," I said.

"What?" she asked.

"I'm not looking at you," I said. "You're being bossy."

"You know I'm right," she said. "Stop being a baby."

Putting my hands away from my eyes, I looked at her again. "Oh, okay," I said, and we walked up the stairs. I rang the doorbell. I didn't even practice what I was going to say. I was just going to say "sorry" and be done with it. What else could I do? There was no more trash to clean up. Her porch looked clean enough. There was no answer. "Good," I said to Chris and started to walk away. "She's not home."

"Come on," Chris knocked on the door. "This is probably what Santa was talking about." There was no answer. "I've never seen her not home," she said and peeked in the front windows. "I see her on the chair." She knocked again.

"She's taking a nap," I said. "Wow who's worse, me for doing the trash thing or you for waking her up."

"Seriously," Chris said. "Listen to yourself. Maybe something is wrong." She tried the door handle and it was open. "It's open," she said.

"Oh great," I said. "Now who's worse? Breaking into her house?"

"Shut up," she said. "What if something's wrong?" she walked into the house. "Hello? Mrs. Green? It's Chris, remember me?" she turned to me and said, "My mom and dad come to visit her sometimes."

"You didn't tell your parents what I did, did you?" I asked.

"No way," she said. "That would be too embarrassing for me!" We sneaked quietly over to the chair. "Hello?" Chris said. "Mrs. Green?" The old lady was sitting on a chair with the television left on. She didn't move. It didn't even look like she was breathing. We stood there for a minute.

"She's not up," I said.

"Go tap her on the shoulder," she said.

I shuffled past Chris to stand closer to Mrs. Green and tapped her on the shoulder. Suddenly her eyes popped wide open and she let out a gasp. I jumped back and Chris jumped a little too.

"What are you doing?" Mrs. Green yelled.

"We thought you were dead," I said.

"Dead?" she said. "Maybe I would be if you keep sneaking up on me like that."

Chris stepped up and said, "Hi, Mrs. Green. It's me, Chris. My parents come visit you. We knocked and rang the doorbell but you didn't answer. We're sorry we startled you."

"It's okay," she said. "It's okay."

We stood there for a moment. I don't know about Chris, but I was scared to move. I was scared to leave and scared to stay.

"Do you need something, Mrs. Green?" Chris asked. "Are you all right?"

"Oh, I don't know," she said. "I've got no power to stand up."

"Do you want us to get our parents or call an ambulance—anything?" Chris asked. How did she know all the good things to say, all the kind things to say?

"I don't know," she said. "Listen, I need help with two things. Can you help?"

"Sure," I said.

"First, I need to water my flowers," she said.

"Okay," I said and was more than willing to leave and water those flowers. Chris pulled on my arm, forcing me to come back in front of Mrs. Green.

"I'll do that for you, Mrs. Green," she said and walked out the front door.

Mrs. Green smiled. "Thanks, sweetheart," she said. "Now the next thing maybe you can help and maybe not."

"Sure," I said. "What is it?"

"I've got this thing but I don't know what to do with it," she said. "It's in a white envelope over there."

I went to the desk she was pointing to and found the white envelope. I brought it back to her. She told me to open the envelope, and I found a CD of Christmas music.

"Do you have anything to play that on?" she asked.

I smiled and said, "Yes I do."

Running out the door, Chris was watering flowers and said, "Hey where are you going?"

"I'll be right back," I said. "You won't believe what she needs."

After getting the CD player Santa left me, I brought it back to Mrs. Green's house. I set it up and opened the CD, and we all listened to it. Christmas music filled the room. "Peace on Earth and mercy mild; God and sinner reconciled…" My heart began to get lighter, less heavy with the burden over what I'd done. It felt good to help Mrs. Green. I know I'd make Santa proud.

"Well," I said, "we should get going now."

"Wait a minute," Mrs. Green said. "Can't you stay a little? I've got cookies and milk in the kitchen."

Chris pulled me aside. "She's lonely," she said. "We should stay."

"Okay," I said. We went to the kitchen. Chris checked to find the milk she had was sour. There were no cookies. In fact, there wasn't much of any food there.

"My parents bring her some groceries sometimes," Chris said. "But I'm sure they didn't even know it was this bad."

"I'll take a couple of cookies," Mrs. Green said from the other room.

"She's probably hungry," Chris said.

"You stay here," I said. "I'm going to make her some soup! It's what my mom makes when I don't feel good."

Chris smiled at me like she never had before. What I wouldn't do to keep her smiling at me like that. "That sounds great, Travis," she said.

"I'll be right back," I said as Chris sat with Mrs. Green.

My mom helped me make some soup. I told her it was for Mrs. Green. "Is she all right," she asked me.

"I guess," I said. "She's just hungry."

TEN

As I left with a pot of soup and pack of crackers, my mom was putting her nurse scrubs on to get ready for work. "I'm going to stop over and see if she's all right in a minute, sweetie," she said to me.

I carried the soup as carefully as I could to Mrs. Green's house. Just as I was approaching her porch, who walks up. Dirk. He stood in my way.

"What do you want, Dirk?" I said. "I got to go get this soup to Mrs. Green."

"Soup?" he asked. "Is that what this is?"

"Yeah," I said. "Now move."

"Something nice for the old lady, huh?" he asked. "Was this your little deal with Santa? Huh? Help out the old lady, get on the nice list, get that Z-Box?"

"Shut up, Dirk," I said. "And get out of my way." My heart was starting to pound, my head was starting to burn. It was hard not to put the soup down and punch him.

Dirk pushed me. "You traitor," he said and knocked the soup right out of my hands. It crashed on Mrs. Green's steps with soup all over the place.

I couldn't tell you what happened next or how I did it, but my head felt like it was going to explode. First, I picked up Dirk and carried him to a telephone pole nearby. There I pushed him up against the pole and kept doing it even though he was crying. I yelled, "You jerk! That soup was for Mrs. Green. You big jerk!"

He was crying as I kept pushing him up against that telephone pole.

"Stop," he said. "You're hurting me."

I let him go, and he fell to the ground. "I never want to see you again."

Just as he was running away, my mom ran up. "What's going on, Travis?" she asked.

I don't know why, but I just started crying—worse that Dirk. I hoped he didn't hear me, but he was so far away I don't think he did. "He knocked the soup out of my hand," I said. "And I just couldn't stop beating him up."

My mom held me. "It's okay," she said. "Stay away from that kid."

Just then Chris appeared at Mrs. Green's door. "Hey guys," she said, "Mrs. Green doesn't feel good."

We ran up to the front door, making sure not to step on the soup. My mom went in first. Mrs. Green sat quietly, not being able to move. "Sweetheart," my mom said, "how are you?"

"Tired," she said.

"What's your name?" mom asked.

"Mrs. Green," I said.

"No, I'd like her to say it," mom said.

"Sybil," she said. "Sybil Green."

"Okay," mom said. "Can you get up and come with me to the hospital? Are you strong enough to walk?"

"I can walk," Mrs. Green said.

"Okay, well I'm going to pull my car around," mom said. "Let's get you to the hospital and have you checked out. Okay? You guys stay here, I'll be right back."

My mom left to get her car, and Chris said, "I love your mom."

"Yeah," I said. "Me too." And I thought about Dirk and how he treated his mother. I'll never hang out with him again. In fact, I'll never hang out with anyone who isn't nice to their parents. Well, okay some parents can be mean, but I'm still not going to hang out with someone who is mean to their parents—even if they deserve it.

The door opened again and my mom came in. "Okay," she said. "The car is right outside. Are you okay to walk, Sybil?"

"Yes," she said. And my mom helped her up. Chris and I helped too, but my mom really got her toward the front of the house. We walked her down the steps and Sybil saw the soup.

"What happened here?" she asked.

"I spilled some soup," I said. "I'm sorry."

Mrs. Green stopped and looked up. "You're already forgiven, for any spills you've made—both in the past and this one." She winked at me. She turned to my mom and said, "You've raised a fine young man."

"I agree," my mom said and gently helped Mrs. Green in the car and closed the door.

"Is she going to be all right?" I asked.

"She needs some food and water," mom said. "And she needs to be looked over. I think she's going to be fine. She's lucky to have you two. You may have saved her life." She gave us both a kiss on the forehead and got in her car.

As my mom drove off, I looked down at the soup. "I've got to clean this up," I said.

Chris stood there for a moment, looking at me. I'm not sure why. Then she hugged me! Just like that. I didn't know what to do. She was crying a little. "What's wrong?" I asked and hugged her back.

"I don't want her to die," she said.

"Not if my mom can do anything about it she won't," I said. "Now let's clean up this soup."

We cleaned up the soup. Later, Chris helped me write this note to Santa:

Dear Santa,

I'm not sure if you remember me or not. I'm the kid who tried to kidnap one of your elves. Well, I guess you probably remember that. Anyway, I think I got the second chance you told me about. I guess I'd still like a Z-Box, but I understand if I'm off your list. I would like to tell you about Mrs. Green. I think she was my second chance. And

I get what you meant about praying. I pray for her every day. I hope she's okay. Anyway, I've always believed in you. Thank you for believing in me.

Love,
Travis

ELEVEN

Travis Johnson's Testimony, Part 7 of 8: Moment of Truth

A year went by, and it was Christmas Eve again. A lot happened during that year. Dirk never spoke to me for that year, so that's a good thing. He would pass me in the hallway and look the other way. Mrs. Green was okay, but she needed to move to another home where someone could look in on her. My mom said Chris and I could visit whenever we wanted. She didn't have any children or grandchildren, so she was always happy to see us. We've seen her a few times since she moved in. She's very thankful when we visit. I gave her my CD player as a gift.

Mrs. Green never did tell my mom about the trash I dumped on her front porch. Sometime during the summer, after we visited her the second or third time, I told my mom what happened. "Well, you saved her life," mom said. "You made up for it." That removed any bad feelings I had about the whole thing. Mom forgave me, Mrs. Green forgave me. Now would Santa?

It was now Christmas Eve and I was trying to stay awake by our tree. My mother was on the late shift, so my aunt across the way checked in on me and went to bed. Cookies were out, milk was ready. He already must have gotten my note so no sense leaving out anything. "It's now or never," I said to myself and waited. My sleep was light, I didn't want to miss him. Soon, about two o'clock in the morning, there was rustling by the tree. Immediately, I rose from the sofa and turned on the lights.

"Honcho!" I shouted.

"Travis," he said. "Shouldn't you be asleep."

"I was hoping you'd come," I said. "Or someone would come. But wait, aren't you the elf who takes away toys?"

"Yeah, well, what can I say? Big Nick had a change of plans with the whole repo elves program. It's on hold for a little while."

There was a box under the tree. "So what's that?" I asked about it.

Honcho moved to see the box. "What do you think?" he asked and smiled. He reached out to pick it up and hand it to me. "You earned it, kid."

A voice came from toward my bedroom. It was Dirk.

"Nobody move," he said, and he was holding a can of pepper spray. "Don't touch that Z-Box."

Rolling his eyes, Honcho said, "Kid you're like a bad penny. Don't you have a home?"

Dirk walked closer toward the tree, saying, "Nobody move."

"How did you get in here?" I asked.

"Fire escape," he said. He turned to Honcho and held the spray up higher.

"Again with the pepper spray," Honcho said. "Where do you get a hold of that?"

"My brother," he said. "So this is it, huh? Play nice with Santa and get the real goods. You had this in your plans all along."

"You've been planning to sneak in here Christmas Eve for a year, Dirk?" I asked. "Really for an entire year?"

"Not really," he said. "I put it out of my mind till about November. That's when I start seeing all these commercials for the Z-Box. Then I start thinking how you cheated me out of a thousand of these." He turned to Honcho again and waved the spray. "Back away," he said. He got to the gift and opened it. "Well, well, guess what I got now?" It was a Z-Box.

Gold snowflakes filled the room, then another voice. "That's not the way you get presents from Santa, Dirk," Santa said.

"It's you," Dirk said. He nearly dropped the box, but he definitely let the spray down. He quickly lifted it again. "I just want the Z-Box, and I'll leave. You owe me that since this one," he said pointing to Honcho, "stole my scooter."

"Can I ask you one question, son," Santa said to Dirk. "What are you afraid of?"

Dirk was startled, "What?"

"What are you afraid of, son," Santa repeated.

Dirk thought for a second. "Not you," he said. "Not any of you."

"Fair enough," Santa said. "Are you afraid of anything?"

"No," Dirk said, "not really."

"Not really?" Santa asked. "Then you must be afraid of something. The dark? Snakes? High buildings?"

Dirk snickered, saying, "No, not any of those things."

"What about being alone?" Santa asked. "Or being powerless? Or being defeated?" Santa asked.

Dirk waited before responding. "This Z-Box is mine," he finally said, "I deserve it."

Santa said, "The only remedy for greed is charity."

He ran toward the door with the Z-Box, but Honcho lunged myself in front to block him. He looked trapped for a second. He ran for the fire escape. He went down two steps but slipped on a small patch of ice. He lost his can of pepper spray but not the Z-Box. He got up and continued running until he slipped again and this time he dropped the Z-Box. He slid through the railing and grabbed the edge of one rail with five floors below his feet. He held on as he watched the Z-Box slide to the edge of the fire escape landing. It dangled on the edge—as he was—with a long fall below.

I headed down the steps. "Hold on," I yelled. "I'm coming."

"I can't hold on," Dirk cried, "it's too cold."

Climbing down the stairs a little slower, I went past the Z-Box and brushed up against it. It slid off the landing a little more. I looked at it and didn't want it to fall. But Dirk called out for help. I couldn't see Santa or Honcho.

As I moved away from the Z-Box it started to fall. Just then, Dirk let go. His scream could be heard all over the neighborhood as he fell. I looked down, and suddenly Santa appeared below. Dirk and the Z-Box both hung in the air for a moment then both lightly touched down on the sidewalk below.

"Even with a thousand gifts, the selfish demand," said Santa. "In all my years, I never know how to handle the incurably self-centered. Can't ignore them. Can't give them coal. Can't lecture them. The worst part about takers like you, Dirk, is that you feel you're entitled to take and take and take. The only time you give is when you know that somehow you'll be able to take. You nearly lost your life here tonight, yet I can bet that you don't see it that way. I bet you see it that you deserved to be saved and that you still deserve that Z-Box. You don't." When Santa said this, the Z-Box floated in the air to where I was sitting on the fire escape. "But do you know what you deserve?"

"No," Dirk said.

"The greatest gift of all," said Santa. "Do you know what that is?"

"No," Dirk said again.

"A second chance," he said.

"Second chance at what?" Dirk asked.

"You're smart," Santa said. "You'll figure it out. Now go home, and be thankful."

Dirk looked around a little then up at me, and then he ran off.

Santa and Honcho looked up at me and smiled. Gold snowflakes swirled around them and suddenly they were both gone.

Twelve

Honcho told me about the problems in the North Pole. There are kids believing in Santa as they get older, like I did. That was the reason he took back toys. I understand why you started doing that, and also why you decided to stop doing that. I also know that older kids want the better presents, like cool Z-Boxes and all that. But there is something else I learned from all this. It's like my mom says, "It's better to give than to receive." I felt happier making up with Mrs. Green, then making her happier by visiting her and giving her a drawing that I made just for her or some other gift. Once Chris gave her an ornament that she made. Mrs. Green loved that.

Let us kids believe in you, Santa. Let us believe for as long as we want. The day we stop believing is a sad day. It's like losing your first tooth or your first day of school. It's a big deal. So let us hold on as long as we can.

Nobody said you have to keep giving us presents. In fact, that's probably the worst thing you can do. It's only going to make us selfish like Dirk and want even more. The more you get, the more you expect to get. The more you give, the closer you get to happiness. At least that's what I've found. Stop giving us presents and make us start thinking of the gifts we should be giving to others. Then we become like you, Santa. And don't you want more helpers?

Helpers make the world a nicer place to live.

THE END

Parental or Older Sibling Appendix Report:

Illustrations to Help Your Children Understand about the Repo Elf Squad

Artwork by Tony Perri

The following pages contain illustrations and captions you can use to teach your children about this story. The images depict important scenes from the testimony given by Honcho, Santa, and Travis. This will help your child or younger sibling recognize that Santa only values authentic niceness. These drawings should stress the importance of being nice—not simply acting nice.

Travis was the first kid to attempt to trap one of Big Nick's elves—with the help of Dirk, of course!

Honcho, left, and Sequence lead Big Nick's special forces—
the one he deploys after Christmas.

With a wave of his hand, Big Nick sent everybody out of the room—
except Travis. He had a special message for him.

Travis wanted to know why he needed a second chance. Chris reminded him that he was the one who trashed Mrs. Green's porch.

Dirk was on the top of Honcho's list of N2N Hackers. He was priority one on the gift repossession schedule—and the only kid to hack the Nice List twice!

Travis couldn't believe his eyes! He had actually caught an elf trying to take back his gift!

Charge, Santa's right-hand man.

"Well, somebody's got to make the tough decisions around here," Big Nick barked at them. "You all sit around here with your red noses and rosy cheeks, yucking it up."

"You're not the ones who put it on the line, zapping your strength and magical powers every day to make this happen."

Honcho twisted Charge's tie and said, "If I don't get fed soon, I'm not going to be nearly as cute."

Dirk came up with a great idea to get Travis in trouble with Big Nick—and it had to do with Mrs. Green.

Repo Elf.

You'd better watch out!

By TOM SIMS   With illustrations by ANTHONY PERRI

Printed in the United States
By Bookmasters